For Seán
D.D

For Maria
M.E.

Macmillan Publishing Company
866 Third Avenue
New York, NY 10022

Maxwell Macmillan Canada, Inc.
1200 Eglinton Avenue East
Suite 200
Don Mills, Ontario M3C 3N1

First published in 1991 by Piccadilly Press, Ltd., London,
England as The Big Lie

First American Edition

Printed in Hong Kong.

10   9   8   7   6   5   4   3   2   1

The text of this book is set in 14 point Novarese Medium.
The illustrations are rendered in watercolors.

Library of Congress Cataloging-in-Publication information is available.

ISBN 0-02-726360-6

The Walking Catfish

by David Day

illustrated by Mark Entwisle

MACMILLAN PUBLISHING COMPANY · NEW YORK

MAXWELL MACMILLAN CANADA · TORONTO

MAXWELL MACMILLAN INTERNATIONAL · NEW YORK · OXFORD · SINGAPORE · SYDNEY

NOBODY. Not nobody, not never, no time and nowhere told bigger and better lies than my friend, Hank Blizzard. It was a matter of considerable pride to our hometown of Archie's Bottom that everybody up and down the whole river knew that Hank was the best.

Bein' an orphan adopted by poor folks, nobody really knew where Hank got his talent from in the first place. All they knew was that real big lies had been coming out of his shaggy, straw-haired head ever since he could talk.

Hank was the one that really made us the most fearsome gang when it came to the Big Lie Competitions. When I say us, I mean the River Rat Gang, 'cause that's what we called ourselves.

Besides Hank, we had Jimmy Joe who could lie pretty good, and outspit just about anybody. Then we had Fat Frankie whose daddy was notable as the best bootlegger in the county, and Tom Curley whose great-grandaddy was the first riverboat pirate to ever settle in Archie's Bottom.

We also had one girl, named Annie Archibald, who had more freckles than any other human being alive. Then there was me: Lee Roy Jones, except on account of being too young, I wasn't considered a full-fledged River Rat. But I was working on it.

Anyway, that day we're all gathered in Gunther's General Store for the Big Three Day Lie-Off. Old Woody Gunther himself is banging his cracker barrel on the head with a hammer, and calling the contest to order.

Now, we may be feeling cocksure about this competition, but we're not fool enough to think the other gang is going to lay down and play dead.

This gang is made up of one mountain boy named Jethro, one timber town kid called Spike, another kid in a cowboy hat and boots with silver spurs called Tex, and two full-blooded Indians called Duke and Butch.

They are known as the Road Dog Gang. And they travel about with their namesake, which is a beat up, mean-lookin', dirt-colored mongrel of a hound dog.

This bein' the first day of the Lie-Off, you'd have thought everybody would start up kind of cautious-like, but inside fifteen minutes the air is so blue with lies you can't hardly see the other side of the store.

There are stories about mosquitoes so big they carry off cattle and children. Heat waves so hot, the chickens lay hard-boiled eggs, and corn fields produce popcorn.

There are stories of rainstorms so bad that frogs drop out of the sky, and windstorms so fierce they blow the feathers off of chickens, the fur off of cats, and houses into the next county.

Fat Frank tells one story about a man who suffered from spontaneous inflation.

Annie Archibald tells another about a local artist who made a picture of a wolf so lifelike, the critter chewed up his paintbrushes.

That mountain boy Jethro brags about a hunter from his parts, who's so strong and mean, he can reach down a mountain lion's throat deep enough to grab hold of its tail and pull the critter inside out.

After this one, Woody Gunther starts to bang his hammer on top of his crackerbarrel to call us to order.

"I declare the first day of the Three Day Lie-Off at a close," Old Man Gunther says in his most official voice. "Some real whoppers been told, but I reckon everyone would agree it's pretty much a draw so far."

So, we're into the second day. The Road Dogs come out with such a heap of scorchin' hot lies that the paint is blistering on the store walls, and Old Woody is complaining that all the labels are peeling off his fruit and fish cans.

It's past the middle of the afternoon, and I hate to say it, but those Road Dogs are making us look real bad. There's only time for one more whopper. So we know it's up to Hank to come up with a real zinger to save the day.

But Hank never gets flustered. He just stands up and commences to speak his piece about a catfish that lives hereabouts that's so big and mean it walked right out of the river and swallowed up several river bottom fishermen.

Now this seems pretty tame stuff to the Road Dogs, and they say so. "Pitiful," says Spike. "What kind o' lie you call that?"

"I don't call it any kind o' lie at all," says Hank. "It's the plain simple truth."

"Stupid," says Butch.

"Is you callin' me a liar?" Hank shouts at the Road Dogs.

Now, Old Gunther takes notice, because this is against the rules. Nobody in a Big Lie-Off can call the other a liar, unless they risk penalty points by calling on the other team to prove their story's true.

But the Road Dogs just laugh, and Tex Silver Spurs shouts, "Yeah, we are calling you a liar and a bad one at that. So show us your walking catfish, you yellow-bellied river rodent."

"Well, it just so happens," smiles Hank, "Fat Frank and me caught a small one trying to break into the chicken coop last night."

Hank picks up a bucket with a heavy wood lid on which he's been sitting all the while. He lifts the lid and dumps the bucket, water and all, onto the wooden slat floor of Gunther's store. And in the middle of the floor in a pool of water is this mean-lookin' catfish, about one foot long, flip-flopping back and forth.

Everybody from both gangs is looking at this critter. It's a catfish all right, but it isn't like any catfish I've seen before. It's got these stubby little flippers on each side.

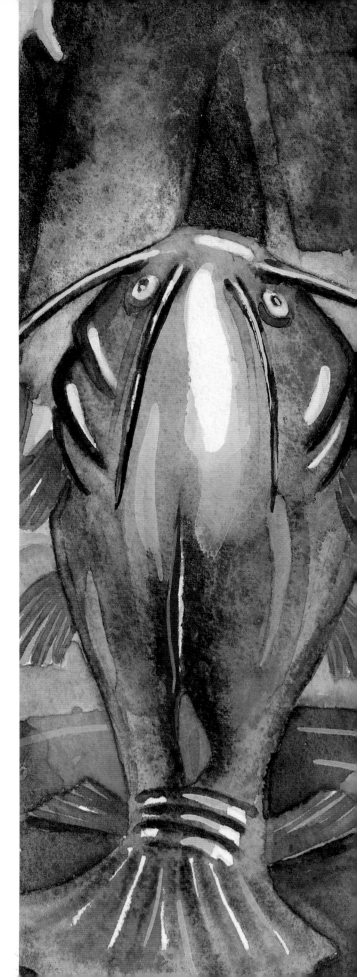

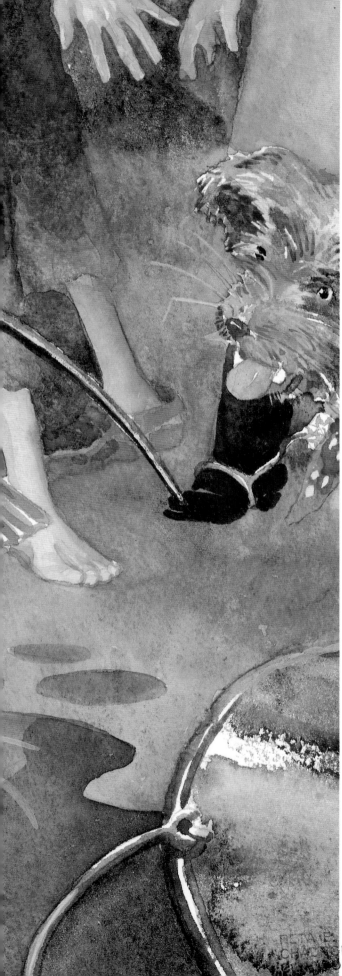

All of a sudden, it sort of stands up on those stubs. Then it twists and kind of leaps forward a ways and starts to make a fishy walk across the floor. It heads directly toward the Road Dogs, who're standing there with their mouths wide open.

There is no doubt about it. This is a living, breathing – and more to the point – WALKING catfish.

This, Hank explains, is a catfish that comes from a place called Siam, which is like China only south a ways. And it turns out all the catfish there can walk around. Anyway, somebody brought some over here and dumped them in some canals, and a few years back some came up our river.

So Gunther looks at the Road Dogs, and says, "Sorry boys, but you lose a whole bunch of points on account of being suckered in and callin' Hank a liar on a true story."

At that Woody Gunther's hammer hits the barrel head to close the day's competition.

The Road Dog boys don't know where to look. There's no use denying this is a walking catfish. It does its wiggly walk right up to their mangy old hound dog, which starts to snarl at this uppity fish.

All of a sudden, fur and scales are flying, and there in the middle of the floor in Gunther's store is the meanest catfish-dog fight ever seen in Archie's Bottom.

That catfish just takes a big bite right into the dog's snout, and the hound is hurling itself about the store. Yowling and snarling, the dog crashes out the door into the street. Finally, after racing up and down the road for some time knocking down furniture and townfolk, that old dog just runs straight off the dock at the end of the street, and throws itself into the river.

O' course, this is just what the catfish is waiting for, and he lets go of the dog's snout and swims himself off.

That poor old hound is left to drag himself up out of the river, looking downright humiliated at being outfought and outsmarted by a fish. And with us jeering and hooting, the Road Dog Gang looks pretty much like their own whipped hound.

"It may be a walking catfish, and it may even be mean enough to take a nip out of a fisherman," shouts Spike, "but there ain't no way it's big enough to swallow a man."

"Well," says Hank, "This is only a baby one, but like I said, there's one grown to the size of three grizzly bears, with an appetite to match."

But the Road Dogs still don't put much stock in Hank's story.

So Hank dares Tex Silver Spurs to meet him and Fat Frankie at the dock at first light tomorrow morning. Then they'll take him downriver a piece so he can see the monster catfish for himself.

The Texan Road Dog says he's willing, so they spit and shake on it.

Next day we're all gathered at the store again. Well, all of us, 'cept Hank, Frank, and Tex, who are nowhere to be seen.

Just then, Hank comes screaming and howling up the street. He looks like he's scared to death and is soaking wet. His face is all white, and Frank's mother and several townfolk are hot on his trail.

"The Catfish!" Hank yowls, "The Catfish!"

And Fat Frank's mother is screaming as well, "Frankie's gone, Frank's drowned. And that boy, Tex Silver Spurs, too!"

It's a considerable time before the full story comes out.
But it appears that the monster catfish suddenly came up
after the boys and swallowed both Frankie and Tex, all in
one piece.

By now the entire population of Archie's Bottom is either
running along the riverbank or out in boats, looking for the
boys.

Hank's old rowboat is flipped over and nearly chewed in
half in the river, and Tex's Stetson can be seen floating
nearby. Later, a little way downstream, a chewed up strip of
Frank's shirt is found, along with one of Tex's boots.

"I thought you just went and made up that story about how big that fish was, Hank," whispers Annie with her eyes wide open.

"So did I," howls Hank out loud, "but my story just came to life and ate up Fat Frankie and Tex. It's all my fault. It's a judgement on me. The preacher told me, one of these days, one of your big lies is going to come back and get you. Well, it sure enough did. Looks like Lucifer himself has become a catfish and come after me, 'cept he missed, and took Fat Frank and the Texan instead."

It looks for a while like Hank might go crazy right there, or take up religion, or some other fool thing.

He falls down on his knees, and prays out loud.

"Lord, forgive me. Lord, bring back Fat Frankie, and even that lying Road Dog boy, too. Oh Lord, I'm sorry for my sinning ways."

Then just in the middle of one of Hank's prayers, one of the Road Dogs, who till now've been wailing away like everybody else, starts shouting.

"Hold on! Who's that over cross the river?"

And who should it be, but Tex Silver Spurs standing barefoot and bareheaded in the eel grass and looking across at all the commotion.

A few seconds later, Fat Frankie comes running up, out of breath and looking kind of embarrassed.

It turns out Hank took Silver Spurs to a shack about a mile downriver, and got Fat Frankie to sit on him for a few hours. Meanwhile, Hank took away Tex's hat and boots, threw them in the river, and then broke up his own old rotten boat and let it float around upside down.

But after a while the Texan wriggled away from Fat Frankie and ran back up river and, of course, Fat Frankie couldn't catch up.

All through this confusion, with people shouting and wailing, Hank is laughing. He's laughing so hard he falls over backward, then he rolls over on his belly and continues to laugh and is almost hanging over the riverbank still a-laughing.

Seems no doubt now we are going to win the Big Lie-Off hands down on sucker points, but maybe Hank's gone more'n a little too far on this one. Folks are grumbling and looking ugly.

Even Old Man Gunther, who can appreciate a great lie when he hears it, just moves off feeling like Hank's gone and double-crossed everybody in Archie's Bottom.

Everyone's gone now, 'cept for me and the dog.

"Well, I've done it," crows Hank. "I told a story that swallowed up a whole town, just as sure as the Bible tells how the whale swallowed up Jonah.

"Yes sir, yes siree! I'm willing to wager that one o' these days I'll out-lie old Lucifer himself, if the good Lord will only arrange for the meeting."

These words are just out of his mouth when something monstrous, huge and black, comes exploding up from the river bottom and bursts out onto the bank next to Hank.

It's a giant, black, slimy, walking catfish the size of two tractors! And before I can say a word, or the hound can howl, it pounces forward on its walking fins and swallows up Hank in a single gulp.

After that, it just slips back down into the river, and it's gone.

All that happened a considerable number of years back now.

But I tell you, when I got into town shouting and screaming for all I was worth, with that scared hound howling behind me, I couldn't find anybody who was willing to believe me.

O' course, I didn't have the sense to shut up. I kept on telling folks the story. Over and over. After a while, people took to calling me "Catfish" Jones.

I suppose I'll still be telling the story when I'm ninety, but now I know nobody's ever going to believe me.

The townfolk have flat out refused to hold a funeral. They say that's just what Hank wants. They say he's hiding out in the hills, just waiting for the day when he can turn up at his own funeral. But they are bound and determined to outwait him.

There are some days when I wonder about it myself. There are rumours from time to time that come drifting down from the hills. Maybe, just maybe, if I could persuade folks to have the funeral, Hank would actually turn up.